The Mermaid's Tail

Raewyn Caisley

Illustrated by Ann James

SCHOLASTIC INC.

New York   Toronto   London   Auckland   Sydney
Mexico City   New Delhi   Hong Kong   Buenos Aires

To all my Cronulla mermaids

— *R.C.*

Love & splashes for Finola

— *A.J.*

ISBN 0-439-40497-5

12 11 10 9 8 7 6 5 4 3 2 1   2 3 4 5 6 7/0

Printed in the U.S.A.   40
First Scholastic printing, October 2002

Chapter One

Crystal had been a fairy
once, but that was when she
was only three. Now that
she was older, she knew
what she was going to be: a
mermaid!

She did everything she could to make it happen. She swung her legs under her chair while she had breakfast. Then she walked with tiny little steps when she got down from the table.

"I'm a mermaid," she said to Mom and Dad.

"Well, you've got the right hair for it," said Mom.

Dad had once said her hair reminded him of

seaweed. Now she didn't
mind that at all!

At the beach, she swam
with her ankles together,
until her anklebones got too

sore. Then she sat on a rock
and combed her hair. She
used the comb Mom kept in
her swimming bag. It
was old and yellow, and it
looked like fish bones.

Crystal held her breath in the bathtub to see how long she could stay underwater.

"Don't do that," said Dad.

She even tried to fit both legs into one side of her green pajama pants, and every night, before she went to sleep, she made a very special wish.

"I wish I were a mermaid," she said with her eyes shut very tightly.

But no matter how many
things Crystal tried,
nothing she did ever
seemed to work.

"What do I have to do
to be a mermaid, Mom?" she
asked one night.

Mom helped her put her
pajamas on the right way.
Then she gave her a kiss
and tucked her in.

"You leave that to me,"
said Mom.

Chapter Two

Mom made clothes for a
booth she had at the Sunday
flea market.

She made crumpled skirts
that opened up like fans.
She made puffy pants that

filled up like balloons. They
had rainbow colors, tinkling
bells, stars, moons, and
feathers.

Crystal loved the things
Mom made.

"Wake up, Crystal," Dad
called out on Sunday
morning. "Mom's got a
surprise for you."

She ran into Mom and
Dad's room and climbed into
their big bed.

"Mom's been up half the
night," said Dad.

Mom yawned and took something out of her sewing bag. She stretched it around Crystal's waist and said, "I hope it fits."

Crystal was so happy she couldn't think of what to say. While she had been asleep last night, Mom had made a mermaid tail.

Chapter Three

She put the tail on.
It was nice and tight, and
there was a hole at the
bottom for her feet. It was
covered all over with deep
green and blue sequins.

"Come on," said Mom.

"You can leave it on to go to the flea market."

Crystal swung her tail under her stool while she had breakfast. It flashed and sparkled in the morning sun. At the flea market, she walked with tiny steps up and down the rows of booths. People in the other booths all watched and smiled.

When the flea market closed, they packed up and went home. Crystal sat in the front of the van. Dad parked outside their apartment and ran upstairs for his surfboard.

"Time to hit the beach!" he said when he came back.

Crystal played in
the sand that
afternoon while her
mother made her
a seashell top.

"What do you
think of that?" asked
Mom.

They sat together
on a rock to watch
Dad surf.

Then, when it
was nearly dark, Dad

carried Crystal home and
ran a bath. It was almost as

if Mom and Dad had
found her washed up on
the shore.

"Can I wear my tail
in the bathtub?" she
asked. She had her fingers
crossed behind her back.

"I guess it would be all
right," said Dad.

Crystal splashed and
splashed. Water went
everywhere. She let
her hair float all around her

head. She squirted water

spouts as high as she could.

She didn't ever want to
get out of the tub, not even
when the water got cold. But
Mom said she had to get
ready for bed.

She had

prunes on

her fingers

when Dad

lifted her

out.

"Would I

turn into a

real mermaid if I wore my
tail to bed?" she asked.

"I'm afraid it's too wet for
that," said Dad.

Chapter Four

On Monday morning, Mom said Crystal could take her mermaid tail to school.

Crystal showed it off to all her friends at recess. She could tell they wished they

had tails, too. Mrs. Winton,
her teacher, said she was the
first mermaid they'd had at
Shelly Beach Elementary.

Then, Mom and Dad
picked her up after school.
"It's so hot," said Mom.
"I thought we could go to the
pool!"

Crystal's heart jumped. She
imagined the lifeguard
finding a mermaid swimming
around in the deep end.

When they got to the

pool, she quickly ran to get changed. She didn't want anyone seeing her without her tail.

She wobbled out of the dressing room when she was ready.

Crystal stood on the edge of the pool. She took a deep breath. She looked around at the other kids.

"Come on, Mermaid, jump!" said Dad, and Crystal did.

Then, a moment later, she popped out of the water like a cork!

The tail made her feel very brave. She jumped into Dad's arms again and again.

But somehow she couldn't open her eyes underwater.

She stayed in a lot longer than she ever had before. She tried doing forward rolls and back flips, but she couldn't hold her breath for very long.

After a while, she began to feel cold. She made two fists and rubbed her eyes.

"Come on," said Dad. "Time to get out."

"But a real mermaid
wouldn't get out yet,"
Crystal almost cried.

"What's the matter?"
asked Mom.

"It still isn't like being a
real mermaid," said Crystal.

Chapter Five

Crystal hoped that if she
wore her tail long enough
something magical might
happen.

At school, she wore it
during recess and lunch.

At home, she wore it every
night in the bathtub.

She even wore it on Friday to
go on a late-night shopping trip.

Crystal walked with tiny little steps all around the supermarket, but her mermaid tail kept falling down.

"Come on," said Dad. "Do you want a ride?"

She swung her tail onto the shopping cart, but the blue and green sequins kept falling off.

"At least we will find our way home again," Dad laughed.

It was too late for a bath
by the time they got home.

"Straight to bed for you,"
said Dad.

Crystal wriggled carefully
out of her mermaid tail and
hung it on the back of her
bedroom door. Another blue
sequin fell to the floor.
It made her sad.

"Night, night," said Dad.
"Sweet dreams."

She curled her legs up

in the dark and stared out the window at the stars.

She still hadn't worn her tail to bed. Somehow it had always been too wet, but it wasn't tonight.

She didn't think Mom and Dad would mind if she wore it just this once. . . .

Chapter Six

"Ee, ee, ee, ee." Crystal heard a strange sound. She opened her eyes and looked around.

A real, live dolphin was tapping at her bedroom window!

She looked at the floor.
It was covered with sand!
Seaweed was growing
out from under her bed!
A tiny crab was hiding
in the corner under her
dresser!

Crystal pulled back her
blanket and looked at her
tail. It was smooth and wet
and scaly.

She gave her tail a flick. It
didn't fall down. It flashed

and sparkled as if it were made of silver.

Crystal did a forward roll with joy. The dolphin did one at the window.

Just for fun she did a back flip as well. So did the dolphin!

Crystal opened the window and swam out into the ocean. Then, she and the dolphin swam all the way to the top.

Whoosh! They both leapt as high as they could out of the water.

When they came back down, they made an enormous splash. The dolphin clapped his flippers together and made Crystal laugh.

She loved being a mermaid. It was like having a clown at your birthday party, only better.

Crystal flicked her flashing silver tail. She thought she could stay a mermaid forever and ever.

Chapter Seven

Crystal did all the things
she used to imagine herself
doing.

She flopped her tail
around lazily while she had
breakfast. She ate raw

oysters straight out of their

shells!

Then, she wriggled her
tail as fast as she could
when she and the dolphin
went for a swim.

"I'm a mermaid!" she said
to herself.

The dolphin just nodded
his head and laughed. It was
almost as if he knew what
she was thinking.

On the bottom of the
ocean, they played in a
garden of kelp. It swished
and rolled in the current.

Then, they tickled giant
clams with the tips of their
tails.

Crystal squealed when they made the clams snap their shells closed.

They threw colored starfish back and forth to each other as if they were Frisbees.

"Ee, ee, ee, ee," the dolphin said, balancing an orange starfish on his head.

Crystal collected more and more to see how many he could balance.

Then, they flicked their

tails and

swam

away.

Crystal and the
dolphin spent the
whole day playing in
the ocean.

They scattered schools of
glistening fish and flipped
over giant jellyfish.

But then, at last, Crystal
began to feel tired. She
found herself thinking
about Mom and Dad, and
suddenly, she knew she
would miss them too much if

she stayed a mermaid
forever.

The dolphin swam over
and gently nuzzled her
shoulder.

"Ee, ee, ee, ee," the
dolphin said, and somehow
Crystal understood what he
meant.

She looked up and saw
the bottom of Dad's
surfboard floating on the
surface.

Crystal smiled and said
good-bye to the dolphin.
Up and up and up she
swam.

"Hello, little mermaid,"
said Dad.

Chapter Eight

"Hello, little mermaid," said
Dad. "What's happened to
your tail?"

Crystal's mermaid tail
was on the floor.

Dad hung it up on the

back of the door. "I think
your tail's seen better days,"
said Dad.

"Oh, well," said Crystal.
"I don't really mind."

She ran into Mom and
Dad's room and climbed into
their big bed.

Crystal yawned and
stretched her arms up high.

"Mom," she said.

"Hmm?" asked Mom.

"I want to be a butterfly," said Crystal.